1. Under a Leafy Tree

Three babysitters sat round the sandpit under a leafy tree.

Mrs Mackle had Mark. He was asleep in his pram, so he was no trouble.

Jeff had the twins, Josh and Jessie. They kept bashing one another with their little wooden spades, and trying to feed each other things they found in the sand – dead insects, bits of grass, old sweetie wrappers – but they weren't much trouble.

Flora had Frances. Frances kept charging off out of sight in the bushes, and Flora had to keep running off to fetch her back. Frances was more trouble than all the other three put together.

"Worst child I ever had," said Jeff, "was a sniffer. Sniffed all the time. Sniff! Sniff! Sniff! Little pause, then, *Sniff!* I tell you, this child nearly drove me mad."

He darted forward to take a broken end of lolly stick away from Jessie.

"Worst child I ever had," said Flora, "was a fusser. Such a fusser! Fussed if it wasn't the right cup. Fussed if they weren't the right gloves. Fussed if you made the

2

sandwich wrong, or cut it the wrong way. That child was a real pain."

She rushed off to fetch Frances out of the bushes.

Mrs Mackle put out a hand to rock Mark in his pram while she waited for Flora to come back. As soon as Flora was sitting comfortably on the bench again, Mrs Mackle said:

"I've babysat for some horrible children in my time. I had one who tried to strangle the cat, and one who screamed if you tried to make her put on her welly boots. I've had dozens who wouldn't go to bed at the right time. And I've had sneaky ones – children who are perfectly happy sitting in your lap reading books and

4

doing jigsaws, but as soon as they hear their parents coming home, they start to wail and howl and act as if you'd spent the evening beating them."

"Now that is sneaky," said Flora, rushing off to fetch Frances.

"Terrible," agreed Jeff, taking a lump of something nasty off Josh.

Mrs Mackle rocked the pram, and waited for Flora to get back. Then she told them:

"But the worst child I ever had lived in one of those houses over there."

She pointed over the park.

"See the red house," she said. "The one with white windows: 25, Redlands Road. That's where she

lived, the worst child I ever had."

Overhead, in the tree, a few leaves stirred.

Mrs Mackle sighed.

"This was a long time ago," she said. "Three whole years. This child was very young then. She would be older now."

"Tell us about her," said Flora, running off to fetch Frances.

"Yes, tell us," said Jeff, flicking a bit of twig out of Jessie's mouth.

Mrs Mackle rocked the pram till Flora came back again. Then:

"It's a horrible story," she said. "It makes me shiver even to think about it. You're sure you want to hear it?"

"Definitely," said Jeff.

"Oh, please!" said Flora.

"All right, then," said Mrs Mackle. "I'll tell you."

She leaned forward and whispered so softly that only Flora, Jeff and the leafy tree could hear.

"Her name was Susan Solly," she began.

Up in the tree, young Susan Solly, of 25, Redlands Road hugged herself happily and smiled.

2. *Snail City*

"She was a pretty little thing," said Mrs Mackle. "She was a peaceful baby. She grew into a merry toddler, and then into a cheerful little girl. Everyone round here loved babysitting for her. She ate all her supper, and cleaned her teeth without making a big fuss, and went to bed when she was told, just like a perfect angel."

"She sounds *wonderful!*" said Flora, rushing off to fetch Frances.

"I wouldn't have minded looking after her," agreed Jeff, taking Jessie's spade away because she was bashing Josh too hard.

"Wait till you *hear*," said Mrs Mackle, darkly.

She rocked the pram till Flora came back again. Then she carried on.

"Susan Solly liked painting, and doing jigsaws, and watching the telly, and cutting up magazines, and sticking pictures with glue. She liked her woodwork set and she liked helping to cook. But most of all she liked playing in the garden."

Jeff looked over the park towards 25, Redlands Road.

"It's a good garden," he said.

"Bushes and grass. Is that an apple tree by the fence?"

"Yes," Mrs Mackle said. "That's where she liked to play. Under the apple tree there is a wheelbarrow upside down in the long grass, next to the compost heap. The family throw all their tea-leaves and apple cores and carrot peelings and shrivelled-up bits of lettuce onto the compost heap. And once a week Susan's mother waters it down with the hose, to make it rot faster."

"Nice place to play!" sniffed Flora.

"Get a bit messy," agreed Jeff.

"She didn't play *in* it," said Mrs Mackle. "Or *on* it. She played beside it, in the long grass. She liked it there because there was an old log, and mossy stones, and lots and lots of snails."

"Snails?"

"*Snails?*"

"Yes, snails," said Mrs Mackle. "Dozens and dozens of them. Snails love damp places, you see. And they love bits of old salad. So you ask your average common-or-garden snail his opinion, and he'll tell you that a mossy stone next to a log beside an upturned wheelbarrow under an apple tree in the long grass close to a compost heap is about the best place in the world to live. Positively palatial!"

"Fancy!" said Flora, rushing off to fetch Frances.

"I didn't realise," said Jeff, wiping

something rather peculiar and green off Josh's nose.

"Few people do," said Mrs Mackle. "I never knew much about snails till I babysat for Susan Solly. But she spent hours and hours playing with these snails."

"Playing with them?" said Flora, who had come back.

"Yes," Mrs Mackle said. "Playing. She ran snail parties, and snail schools, and snail feasts, and snail races. She made snail patterns (though they got restless and they always moved). And, if it was dry enough, Susan brought out her paintbox and painted the snails' shells the most beautiful colours in her snail beauty shop."

Mrs Mackle smiled.

"It was a regular snail city, next to that compost heap."

The other two were astonished.

"Didn't she hurt them?" asked Flora.

"Never!" said Mrs Mackle firmly. "Not once. She was as gentle as I am with a baby." To prove it, she gave Mark a little rock in his pram. "She picked them up carefully and put them back after a very short while. She always let them glide off if they seemed bothered. She wouldn't even run a little zoo in her snail city because she loved them so much she couldn't bear to think of them trapped in anything. No. Fair's fair. You have to give young Susan Solly

16

her due. She was a perfect angel with the snails."

"What was the problem, then?" asked Flora.

"Yes," Jeff agreed. "How did this perfect angel turn out to be the worst child you ever had?"

"Wait till you hear," said Mrs Mackle, darkly.

Up in the leafy tree, Susan Solly smiled.

3. *Doing what she was told*

"One day," said Mrs Mackle, "I went off to babysit for Susan Solly. It started to drizzle as I walked up her garden path, and it kept on all morning."

"Nice today, though," said Flora, rushing off to fetch Frances.

"Better than yesterday," agreed Jeff, waiting for Flora to come back so they could get on with the story. He spent the time shaking some of the sand out of Jessie's nappy.

Flora rushed back and sat down.

"Go on," she said to Mrs Mackle.

Mrs Mackle went on.

"Susan, of course, had gone out to play with the snails. I could see her through the window. First she fixed up a snail snack, offering them some juicy fresh titbits she found on the very top of the compost heap. Then she organised a Great Snail Expedition through the wet grass and over the mossy boulders. I think they were supposed to be heading for the rosebush, but a lot of them kept straying."

"It must have been a very slow expedition," said Jeff.

"It certainly was. And while it was taking place, the drizzle turned into

raindrops, and the raindrops turned into a downpour. Susan was in her raincoat and hat and boots, but by the middle of the morning she looked soaking wet."

"I would have called her inside," said Flora, rushing off to fetch Frances.

"So would I," agreed Jeff, rescuing a ladybird Josh was trying to pat with his spade.

"I tried," said Mrs Mackle. "I did try. I opened the window and leaned out.

'You'd better come in now, Susan,' I told her.

'Susan, did you hear me?' I asked.

'I don't want to have to tell you again, dear,' I said.

'Come in and we'll watch cartoons. *Snail Show* is on telly next and you know it's your favourite,' I wheedled.

'If you don't come in, I shall have to tell your mother,' I threatened.

'Susan! Come in right now!' I ordered.

'*Susan*!' I yelled.

'If you don't come in right this

minute, I shall come out there and *drag* you in,' I shrieked.

'SUSAN!!! GET IN THIS HOUSE RIGHT NOW!' I bellowed. And I slammed the window shut so hard I broke a pane."

The other two stared. Jeff's mouth had dropped open. Flora looked aghast.

Jeff said, "What happened?"

Mrs Mackle said, "Would you believe it, after all that time pretending she had cloth ears, that cheeky little madam suddenly gave a secret little smile, whispered something to the snails, then stood up and walked, calm as you please, towards the house."

"Doing what she was told at last!" said Flora. (She sounded quite relieved.)

"Wait till you hear," warned Mrs Mackle darkly.

Up in the tree, young Susan Solly gave yet another little secret smile, and hugged herself again.

4. Snail Show

Flora rushed off to fetch Frances. When she came back, she said to Mrs Mackle, "I don't think I would have sat and watched *Snail Show* cartoons with Susan Solly after all that."

"Neither would I," agreed Jeff, prising Josh and Jessie apart because they were trying to bite one another. "I'd have been far too cross."

"I was, too," said Mrs Mackle. "I went straight into the kitchen to make myself a cup of coffee. I didn't even offer Susan orange juice. And she didn't come in and ask for it. She just kept marching back and forth from her toy cupboard under the stairs to the front room, carrying armfuls of tiny plastic chairs from her doll's house."

"A nice change," said Flora. "Playing with stuff from her doll's house."

Mrs Mackle snorted.

"Wait till you hear," Jeff warned Flora, to save Mrs Mackle the bother of saying it darkly. Then he turned to Mrs Mackle. "Carry on."

She carried on.

"I sat at the table in the kitchen, sipping my coffee and nibbling a nice digestive biscuit. After a while, I heard Susan switch on the television in the front room."

"Was it *Snail Show* cartoons?" asked Flora, as she rushed off to fetch Frances.

"Yes," Mrs Mackle told her when she came back. "I recognised the silly song they always sing."

"And did Susan sit and watch it all by herself?" asked Jeff, prising Josh and Jessie apart because they were trying to poke one another's eyes out.

"I thought she did," said Mrs Mackle. "That's what I thought at first. But then, in between sips of coffee and nibbles of biscuit, I thought I heard the back door

quietly open. And quietly close. And open. And close. And open. And close."

"How strange . . ." said Flora.

"Very odd . . ." agreed Jeff.

"Just what I thought," said Mrs Mackle. "So I called out, 'Susan, are you all right, dear?' And she called back, 'Yes, thank you, Mrs Mackle'."

"She sounds like a perfect angel," Jeff said wistfully, prising Josh and Jessie apart because they were trying to pull one another's hair out.

"Wait till you hear," warned Flora, to save Mrs Mackle the bother of saying it darkly. Then she rushed off to fetch Frances.

When she came back, Mrs Mackle took up the tale.

"So I drank up my coffee and finished my biscuit. And just as I was rinsing the cup under the tap, I thought I heard the back door again. Open. And close."

"Weird . . ." Flora said.

"Most peculiar . . ." agreed Jeff.

"So I thought I'd better go and take a look."

"You never know," said Flora.

"Better safe than sorry," agreed Jeff.

"I walked across the kitchen and opened the door. There was nothing in the hall, just the door of the toy cupboard under the stairs swinging open, and Susan's doll's house empty on the floor."

Flora looked round for Frances.

But, tired suddenly from all that running away into the bushes, Frances had climbed quietly into her pushchair, and fallen fast asleep.

Jeff glanced in the sandpit. Josh was squashed up as close to Jessie as he could get, sucking his own thumb but patting Jessie's chubby thigh.

Jessie's eyes were drooping.

"Go on," whispered Flora.

"Yes, go on," whispered Jeff.

"I walked down the hall and pushed open the door of the front room. At first I saw nothing special – just the same old furniture in the same old places, and, on the television, *Snail Show* cartoons blaring away."

"To an empty room?"

"Nobody watching?"

"That's what I thought at first! But then I saw!"

Mrs Mackle's face drained dead white at the memory. Up in the branches overhead, a few leaves stirred as if a breeze had rippled through the tree.

"Saw *who*?" whispered Flora.

"Saw *what*?" whispered Jeff.

Mrs Mackle leaped to her feet, tearing her hair at the memory.

"Dozens of them!" she cried. "Dozens of the horrible, slimy, slithery things! Each one perched on its own tiny plastic doll's chair! Each one with its little head poked out of its shell, and its little horns straining!

35

A whole lot of them, looking for all the world as if they were at a little private cinema, watching a show on the big screen!"

"*Snail Show!*"

"*Snail Show!*"

"It was horrible!" cried Mrs Mackle. "Horrible! Horrible! It was the worst sight that I have ever seen in all my years of babysitting. And if

I live to be a hundred years old,
Susan Solly will always be the worst
child I ever had!"

"There, there," soothed Flora.
"Try and calm yourself. It's all over
now."

"That's right," agreed Jeff. "You
said yourself, all this happened a
long time ago."

He put his arms around the shaking Mrs Mackle as the leaves of the tree overhead rustled gently and, six feet above him, Susan Solly smiled.

"Time to go home," Jeff said. "This afternoon seems to have gone very fast. It's almost tea time."

Pulling her coat around her shoulders, Mrs Mackle slipped the brake off the pram.

"See you tomorrow," she said, and set off for the north gate.

"Cheerio," said Flora, wheeling the pushchair towards the west gate.

Jeff strapped the twins into the double buggy.

"Bye!" he called over his shoulder as he hurried off to the east gate.

38

There was a moment's silence. Then, with a rustle of leaves, young Susan Solly slid easily down the tree trunk and set off, calm as you please, across the park to the south gate and 25, Redlands Road.

She was still smiling.